Orange September

Jasmine Farrell

Table of Contents

11:11 p.m. 1

Silly Lil' Plant Abandons Comfort 2

Chitchat 3

Shyness and Tea 4

It Started Here 5

Surefire 7

You Gon' See 8

Walking Under Water 9

Mutual Thang 10

Déjà Vu 11

Story-Tella 12

Flowers During Yellow August 13

36 minutes (Quickie at Central Park) 14

Thinkin' 'Bout You 16

I Hope I Don't Run Tho' 17

Like Flies to Suga Water 18

But I'm Sayin' Tho 20

'17 Blue 21

Orange September 22

Balance and Good Cookin' 24

Lay Your Armor Down 25

We Ready Now 28

Late Night Shifts in November 29

I Didn't Fall in Love with You 30

We Not U-Haulers but… 31

Pokemynoseinit 32

Gray April 33

We Be Here 35

Scattered Colors and Stuff 36

Articulate 37

Hazy Green during Blue-Sky June 38

Gorgeous June 39

Static 40

Red February 41

Life Goes On 44

Paper Factory Shenanigans 46

Cake at Paesano's 47

Smooth and Resilient 49

T, Da Deep Sea Diver 51

Wet Romantic Strolls 52

Seashore and Sand 53

Maroon March I 55

Maroon March II 56

Maroon March III 57

Soulmate 58

Vegas, Epiphanies, Beige Coils 59

Listenin' to Us 60

886 61

White Bootleg Converses in August 63

LOVE 64

Music and Rivers 65

Even If We Don't Make It 67

Reassurance 68

Winter Letter 69

Dedicated to:

T

Acknowledgements

I would like to thank my honey bun with the extra glaze for their support! Their feedback on the early beginnings of Orange September, their encouragement, post trimmings of this project and simply being them.

I am thankful for all the beta readers and editors who gave their time and energy to Orange September.

I'm thankful for you, the reader. Thank you for reading a piece of my heart, a vulnerable journey to romance and mushy love.

11:11 p.m.

Hands clasping around my favorite porcelain.
Breathing in the steam.
Cheeks embracing the warmth.
Chamomile tea with honey.
Let the stove handle the weight
as I sip in darkness.
Something was supposed to give,
but it wasn't budgin'.
Someone had to surrender,
and I knew it was me.

Comforted by my orange fuzzies, I wiggle
my toes, ready to let go.
Savor my last sip, eyes closed.
Open them to a glowing green
11:11pm on the microwave.

What's next?

Silly Lil' Plant Abandons Comfort

I am like an amaryllis in April.
Out of season, sticking out in a bed of yellow roses.
Silly amaryllis but I'm here.
Ready to show my red petals to flowers I never met.

Never cared much for the unknown.
The uncertainty makes me doubt I can peacefully
open petals unprepared.
But something about this new environment is warm.
Sassy. Fated.
Welcoming to oddly stemmed greenery like me.

Something about this setting is refreshing.
A rainbow January after a December rain.
No.
A rainbow January after a 4-month storm
and I am still in it—
just took a break from it.

I am like a quiet amaryllis
in a crowded plot, surrounded by other creative
plants.

What's that?
Where did this flower come from?

Soothing purple yucca, you intrigue me.

Can you see me too?

Chitchat

Purple dashiki and a soothed stance.
I didn't see you slide into the hall.
Swept up in the chitchat of indie publishing.
Something about recouping funds and
the price of marketing…
Promotion being
an arm, a leg and, a pair of lips.
At least no one has power to tell us shit about how
our cover
should look and how characters
should appeal to the readers.
You chime in with earthy green.
Inquiring about the process, attentive eyes,
intricate details woven into your questions.
I perk up in teal.
Who are you?

Shyness and Tea

You asked if anybody wanted to go to Dunkin'
across the street from the theatre.
I volunteered.

We strolled out in silence,
letting the icy evening take up our space.

I mentioned my favorite tea spots in Harlem.
You provided a few nods, nervous grins my way.

Walking back, nervous grins were smiles;
the nods were engaged stares.

All it took was a lil' awkwardness to
shake off.

It Started Here

My wallet held nothin' but gnats and hope.
All I had was steady movements in the present.
That was enough for you to take me to a show-
I just needed to bring a bottle of Sutter home.
Bustling my way from work
      to the liquor store,
         to the apartment
(Had to freshen up),
           to Greenpoint.
It started here.
Been taking the G train since the 90s—
Never felt so coy to commute than that day.
We met up at the train station and your embrace felt
familiar.
A similar summer softness that saturated my insides
with a placidity I never knew I needed, familiar.
It was quick, but it made sense. It was clear.
Committal confidence that twinged at
the center of my chest from the pull back.
It started here.
We spoke like long-time friends picking up after the
last chitter chatter blast of good-time occasions.
There was no persuasion.

We simply glided up to the surface of whatever this
might be,
whatever we might be.
But I knew this would be a memory that
I'd share over and over decades from now
because…
it started here.

Surefire

I knew.
I knew this love was for a long time,
a lifetime,
forever cackles on benches,
walking far with storytimes loose,
dripping from the roofs of our mouths,
ready to taste each other and *see*.

Initially, I thought friendship.
Even though you had a smile that made me forget
about breathing,
eyes that gave deep suede a good home
to get toasty in.
I thought friendship.

You knew too.
Didn't know what kind of settling
I'd have in your chest;
you knew I'd be settin' pretty, regardless.

We knew.
We just didn't know what kind of knowin' yet.

You Gon' See

I don't believe in love at first sight.
But I do know that
after our unofficial date to the movies,
I already planned on eating your snacks
for the rest of my life.
Got my mouth ready to savor hot kettle corn on the
couch, during movie night.
Tip toeing to the kitchen to chew up some licorice.
Rolling a hard candy in my mouth with my tongue.
I already planned to squeeze that ass even when it has
an AARP membership card in the jean pocket.
First-time lovers?
Nah.
First time I told myself from the beginning, that I'm
trying
to grow old and wise with someone.

Walking Under Water

Long walks through Greenpoint,
tales of your yesteryears lured me in like sirens.
You: initiated a stroll at sunset.
Me: desired more togethered footsteps at night.
We: held our breaths underwater, hoping to hang
around for as long as we could.
I volunteered to be your swooned sea-lady—
Hold the doom tho'.

Mutual Thang

When I wrapped
my pencil arms around you,
I melted into our possibilities and
let the bad what ifs rot (most of them).
Your scent, your essence, your relief,
I held tight with no fear of unrequited anything.
Hot and sticky at the L train station.
I didn't mind though 'cause we both felt the
wiggle of enchantment dancing between us
with the MTA stench.
I instantly craved to submerge into
your story until
The End infiltrated your veins.
In that train station,
Somali-inspired skirt
flying free, whisked away
from silver horses and boiling air,
I was already yours.

Déjà Vu

In an unsolicited fashion, I discovered
an intrusive smile, adorable ears and big brown eyes
that made my heart wander in a way
I'm sure Mama would call
unethical.

But, hey,
when on the road to rediscovery,
facades once sewn on your skin must unravel.
I busted out the seams, risked it all,
showed my ass for folks to kiss.

I swear I've seen this.
I dreamed this.

Story-Tella

Give me your glassy eyes glistening from dancing TV
lights.
As the world turns from auburn afternoon
to navy effervescent eve,
give me your moonshine midnight gin of aches you
refuse to utter.
If you shudder in silence, give me your cold.
I'll remind you of the warmth of your smile,
slip my arms around the girth of your strength.
You've pulled a lot.
You know heavy.
I can carry too.
Give me your heavy sighs due to a society
that overlooks your core for a distant
body they can mold.
I know about mysterious steps onto a path that's dark.
You've seen some things.
You got stories.
I've got them too.
Side by side,
let's share.
You know heavy.
I can carry too.

Flowers During Yellow August

I've received quite a few bouquets of ulterior motives,
dried up *I'm sorrys* with perfume of manipulation,
soft petals of blooming lies,
held up by stems that I'm thankful
never took root in my heart.

       Yeah, I've been given flowers.

But on the last day of a Yellow August,
outside of my job,
you gave me a bouquet of my favorite flowers,
wrapped up in tenderness.
Sparkling, I tasted your lips
and took a whiff of lilies that had
an intoxicating aroma:
           Peace.

36 minutes (Quickie at Central Park)

Lips locked
in a cherry-and-cocoa-flavored makeout session in
Central Park.
Warm sun above us, blanket below.
Fingertips sliding over soft hills,
sensational valleys.
Clutching juicy parts,
tracing the gentle ones.
Heavy breaths, hearts beating against each other.
I love when we're chest to chest.
Those D cups will never not have a resting place on
me.
A few passersby in the distance,
giggling at their inside jokes.
It was almost a private section
of the park for us.
We take a few more steps…
My flowy skirt
covering a moist gem,
craving to feel your touch.
As my brown and black skirt slowly rises up my legs,
tickling my thighs... I beam at the
brown cheeks matching my smile.
Quiet.

Birds chirping.
There's no resistance in being uncouth,
36 winks and a gasp, and not one person
there to bat an eyelash.

Thinkin' 'Bout You

Tell me your dreams.
Release those visions from your lips
as you press your hands against the
table with intensity. Speak on the things you wish to
birth and nurture.
What connections have caused some of your roots to
hesitate nurturing the soil you were born in?
How does your garden still grow sassafras
and a few oak trees despite hurricanes
ransacking your ritualistic maintenance?

Oh, how I want to be yours.
Talk to Mother Nature like she be Auntie.
Your greens are so vibrant, white lilies
so fragile yet—they never wallow wildly in the wind
like the rest of them.
Sturdy and delicate, anchored by divine stems.
Oh, how I want to be yours.

I Hope I Don't Run Tho'

I ain't scared to love.
I'm terrified of the pace.
Slow and steady wins the race,
yet my heart has already decided to stick around
for as long as our four feet walk this ground,
until our eyelids retire from blinking
and, our chest ceases to rise and fall.
I ain't scared to love.
I'm iffy about the risks involved.
I shiver at the thought of a heartache
I'd have to mend.

Like Flies to Suga Water

I never thought I'd be a fly to your
sugar-water-everything.
Your everything gives me a buzz.
I'm bug-eyed-focused
with every syllable of elevation you release,
with every stride towards destiny you take,
with every intention of peace, you create.

I hate when we depart.

Your essence feels like first kisses, midnight munchies,
evening breezes through country windows.
I've told you secrets I've only whispered in pillows.
I'd be content just being a minnow in your waters,
A fly on the wall in the rooms of your heart.

One night, I think the underside of my thoughts
hummed your name
and my frequencies were raised.
I think, when you're around,
my ruminations behave.

I gave you pieces of my run-ons by the water.
You called it laughter and stories.

I mentioned wounds I've only shown counselors,
peeled my shell, let you read lines
I'd never verbalize.

I hope you've realized by now that I'm crazy about
you.
Your quintessence resurrected my love for poetry.
I've become anchored by your persona
and strapped tight to your energy.
Good God, woman, fuck an allegory:
I can't stop thinking about the many
ways I want to make you grin.

'Cause nobody, and I mean nobody,
can entice my soul like you can.
I'm a fly to your sugar-water-everything
You give me a buzz.
I'm bug-eyed, focused on the way you pull me in.
You're not some drug,
King, you're synergy.
You can pull away ego at the seams.
And, T, you have the most beautiful smile I've ever
seen —
Good God, Woman, that smile.
Looks like morning pastries from Princess Bakery,
and I desire to have a nibble of you.

But I'm Sayin' Tho

I am intoxicated by the way your persona sways in
every setting.
Roll my eyes at our parallel weirdness,
bite my lip at the way your mind works.
Can I have your heart for like 50 years?
I promise I won't break it.
I may annoy the fuck out of your
red ticker though.

'17 Blue

It happened a few days
before autumn flew in,
before the methodical migration
of an old journey raised my beak.
It was late summer,
but bravery was right on time.
I submitted to granting this
sterling journey a try.

Uncaging myself from a confinement
that told me I wasn't good enough, was refreshing
and intimidating.

But love gave me wings
to soar above bullshit, and
I was ready to fly even with tears in my eyes.

Orange September

I remember during an orange September,
a solemn sunset was the aftertaste
of conveying a truth, late
to reach my mama.

                                  That's on me.
But I will not apologize for choosing to be free.
Free to love
the way my heart was supposed to.
With wings in shades of red, orange, and black,
a hint of gold.
Free to see the true colors of loved ones
and respect their hues.
I choose to be me.
Late bloomer. Happy about it too.
Right on time meeting the love of my life.
I painted my gray skies blue twice
and wondered why it always rained.
My cue to face my truth
frequently cracked through
my pretend-powder-blue skies.
I'm thankful for the splatter paint.
The pivot.
A reality I thought only existed in the corners
of my thoughts.

I remember during an orange September,
choice sweeping me into a transition
I needed but delayed for years.

Release.
Newness.
Darkness.
Unknown.
Worth. Every. Single. Tear.

Balance and Good Cookin'

Turmeric stains on white pants.
Soul food joint on Fulton to be romanced.
Catfish pieces and sneaky glances.
Steam dances from hot tea.
Turning to the next chapter,
done re-reading pages of faux "happily ever afters."
Learning to let go a little faster.
If only my mind would embrace that truth.

Lay Your Armor Down

To the woman who lights up
every molecule in my being,
ignites the fire burning,
yearning to light
up the world:

Lay your armor down with me.
I have no arrows to bullseye your heart,
no guns with verbal silver bullets
to cease your serenity-glazed glow,
dipped in God's grace
and a ton of arrogance.

I am no villain.

Look within.
Listen to the God you talk to
and He'll confirm it when I say:

You will not discover another heartbreaker ready to
crumble your irrepressibly glowing red.
You will not find that with me.
Calm the past connections that shadow
your epic core.

I am no villain.

You will find a mushy crumb snatcher
making it her mission
to make you smile until NYC strangers think you've
lost your mind.
You will stumble upon a being who wants to make
you grits in the morning.
To the being who can become so vibrant when happy,
nervous, lit, or creative:

Even in your absence you make me quiver.
Make an Esther out of my Queen Vashti havin' ass.
Revive the parts of me I was sure died along with the
poison I chose to drink.
You back bone.
You be like sunshine
when the past overcasts
my vision.
You be like Diggs, I'll be Lathan,
Brown sugar the shit out of this
journey.
You calming chamomile tea
amidst unforeseen hardships.

To the person who makes my root settle like ginger to
chaotic tummies:

Stop frontin' like you don't know you and I are
surefire.
We fit.
We fit.
We fit.
We fuckin' fit.
Cease fumbling your thoughts
on past offenses from bodies, I don't possess.
I am not them.

I fuck up on social cues. Sink my teeth in deep
ruminations of what ifs.
Afraid to give in to the idea that you actually wanna
be there for me.

To the woman who is my mirror with a cock…
To the being who can see me for who I am and refuse
to wear shades…
To the person who can be so pessimistic it makes me
wanna throw glitter on their shoulders, who has more
drive than Bugatti, Ford, and Bentley combined:
I am in love with you.

So, lay your armor down
when you're around me.

We Ready Now

You look at me
like honor sleeps on my shoulders.
I look at you as though lilac skies reside in your eyes.
And,
we don't nervously blink away these days...
A plethora of ways
we love to submerge ourselves in this love…
We ready now.

Late Night Shifts in November

Your hands caress a love story on my frame.
Passion radiates from my pores.
I've never wanted you more.
At least, that's what I always feel
when my body gushes with libidinous, ravenous calls,
waiting for you to feed it.
Eager for your fingers and kisses to leave sticky, sweet
trails.
Providing the perfect position
to reach zenith.

I Didn't Fall in Love with You

I tell people in casual conversation that
I easily fell in love with you.

I didn't.

It wasn't falling.
It was smooth stone,
cool side of the pillow,
vociferous laughter with hints
of frankincense and myrrh.
It was amorous in abundance, and all we needed to do
was
be present.

I didn't fall in love with you.
It was a velvety ride to
luscious kisses, conversations about everything,
doing nasty things in unmentionable places.
It was floating tranquilly to unified grounding,
goal disclosure and bickering about the best
eatery on 14th.
It was us,
doing the easiest, most natural
thing we could do:
Love.

We Not U-Haulers but...

2-months into our relationship,
you asked, "Will you marry me?"
And I said, "Sure, in two years."
But my heart was with the shits right then and there.
Glad we waited though.

Pokemynoseinit

A white January.
A blue sky.
A beige room.
Shades of caramel and mahogany,
tangled under ivory blankets.
        Baby, bashfulness doesn't deserve you.

Your orange is magnetic.

Goodness,
those gorgeous thighs
gift slippery dreams
when I close my eyes.
Your Godiva enticing calves give my lips something
to quiver for.

Your orange is magnetizing.

Hands on *Peek-a-boo*, your grin was enough.
Buttery boldness,
your sunshine smile in white and glistening pearl,
gave me a shyness I knew had a deeper meaning.

Gushy and glorious, you were gracious to gift me
a taste of your purple waters.
A citrus celestial I savored for the first time
but certainly not the last.

Gray April

Ka-ching, ka-ling
Sounds of the J train
plays in the background as my body
surrenders to the sway of its motion.
Humming affirmations to myself,
I'm interrupted by my phone vibrating.

Chatter from high school kids to my left.
A man *Crunchin'* and *smackin'* on a crispy hot sandwich
to my right.
Present on the J, but with you via SMS.
I don't think I've texted so hard, so fast, since.

Bullheadedness and foolish pride on both sides,
we were ready to let this shit go.

That *Ka-ching, ka-ling* lowers, goes mute.
High schoolers' lips moving but not a sound
to be heard.
The man munchin' chews in slow-mo
and all I feel is a pause....

It's over.

Everything is a blur; my heart feels in the right.
Steadfast on remembering the lesson I learned before.
Climbing the stairs, out the Broad Street Station,
I look up at the gray sky.
I will not break the promise I made to myself.
And neither will you break the promise you made to
yourself.
Little did we know, neither of us had to.

For twenty minutes,
we weren't together anymore.
No more us.
The story had ended,
close the book.
Train of love un-boarded us, and
we were left just sitting on opposite sides of the
bench...

And then our souls slapped the shit out of our pride.
We communicated and got back together.
       Just before I started my shift, too.

We Be Here

We got a few stories now.
A handful of,
"Remember that one time?"
and a few cackles in the first chapter.
We be wanderin'.
We be silly in Philly.
Chilly in the Poconos.
Toes in Connecticut Reserves and trails.
Watching wagging tails and open-mouth slumbering
in parks.
We be extra everywhere.
A few stares of the unknown.
We not perfect,
But in this moment,
in this love,
we be here.

Scattered Colors and Stuff

A bad day.
Thoughts.
A collage of
magenta, lavender, mauve, and eggshell,
scattered on a canvas.
You picked me up from work after hearing my strewn
band of fidgety colors during my lunch break call.
A bad day.
Rambling thoughts.
Erratic emotions from past ordeals that I refused to
call out by name.
You whisked me away to Central Park to bury our feet
in the grass and let it all drain out from our toes.
To just breathe, to just release, to just be.
Gray slacks and a floral, ruffled blouse, my feet
relieved to be free
from the black pleather flats I should have thrown
away ages ago.
Grounding with you for the first time was an honor.
Seeing my defined colors again was alleviating.

Articulate

You speak the language of my heart so fluently.

Hazy Green during Blue-Sky June

Baby,
don't look down,
our love has elevated us
to a place that we were craving to reach but too
scared to utter.

Gorgeous June

Oh, golden you are.
A platinum vision you have.
I'd grab the stars if you asked.
Put them in bottle for a minute.
Set 'em free, watch 'em return to the deep blue above
us.
Observe the reflection of the sparkles in your eyes.
Constellations dancing with white shadows in your
eyes. I think I saw a shooting star fall into your
cornea. I'm sure I watched genuine gentleness playing
ring around the rosie behind your irises.
Hot damn, how I love those eyes.

Static

Never afraid of the static
'cause we always land on the right channel.
In sync, ready to convene.
This love was supposed to remain
in my dreams, or so distant relatives say.
So glad I strayed from the *says* and the *well-meaners*.
Relieved you had arms wide-open.
So thankful we chose YES and gave fear no airplay.
We are abundant in courage.
Loving with eyes open and hearts ready to grow
continuously.
We give orange Septembers a long sunset love
and
a tasty white linen, silky sunlit morning.
Fuck no.
I ain't ever scared of the static.

Red February

Girrrrrrl.
Aight, so boom:

T and I went to Roosevelt Field Mall for Valentine's
Day back in '19. They took me to get my ring size,
but they didn't show me the ring (Insert eye roll here,
y'all)!

Anyway, we got a quick bite, took a few pictures
together, and relaxed at the food court. About an
hour later, T walked us over to Small Batch. The
ambiance was set to bougie bedroom eyes, and I was
feelin' it. The overall aesthetic was come-at-able,
lowkey upscale, not chichi-type upscale; you know?

So anyway, after we ordered our food, we observed
the environment and table talked about moving out
of our home city. Oh, and about me being scared to
try their duck. Meanwhile, our ears refused to duck
the married couple that dined at a table next to us.

The woman's essence whispered, "Taste and see."
Eyelashes fanning his way, hoping to cool him off.

The man's essence screamed, "Nah, I'm good. Let me burn."

A few moments into *nom-nom-nomin'* and much-*much-munchin'* T went to the bathroom.

. . .

. . . ..

. . . .

The lady leaned in and asked me how long we'd been together. I awkwardly smiled and scanned her. Face plastered, big and wide. Coraline-fake-mama-button-eyed bright, she was not convincing, but I knew better than to make her feel as though. I told her a little over a year. I couldn't help but simper at the blooming journey.

"That radiant smile tells me you two might be headed for long-term." She nods.

"Yep. Took me to get my ring size today."

The man's head was lowered the majority of the time, as his phone screen highlighted his face in blue and white. White hair, peppered and dry. Cheeks sunken in as if a vacuum took a liking to his face.

He finally looked up, into my eyes and chimed in, "The first two years are amazing. Then it all goes downhill."

His blue eyes spoke of regret and mischievous things. My eyes shifted to his wife's face, and her crazy glue-stuck smile still sat there. She nodded. I muttered, "Hopefully, that won't be the case for ours."

He gave me a hopeful smile, glared at her, and dropped his head back down.

T finally returned. *About fucking time.* I no longer wanted to experience that fuckery alone.

"It's all nice until the love leaves," he spoke once more. This time, he didn't look up from his phone. The duo shared nasty glances and looks. She would cut her eyes quickly and gift him a warning smile. He'd smirk to challenge her. He eventually sat up and jabbed a fork into his plate while glaring at her. She refused to release her gaze from him until after we heard the clink from the fork to the plate.

I texted T what happened so far and filled them in as best I could.

T's face said what my thoughts were sayin: we were in sync, y'all.

The four of us ended up talking about how good the food tasted, how often they've visited Small Batch. For about twenty minutes, T and I kept hearing and seeing the evidence of a possible dumpster fire marriage right next to us.

When we left Small Batch, we told each other that if it ever got even remotely close to that bad to just separate from each other.

Small Batch was delicious though!

Life Goes On

9-5 was 9-5in'
and elbow grease was finna be applied to
my $300 freelance gig.
Nothing stops this phoenix.

Life always goes on.
It keeps moving.

Winter chills whisked up my business casual dress
as I stood in front of my job,
coming from my lunch break.
My stern, my organized,
put-together, two-braided, sides smoothed right-
gathered
had unraveled.
My always-well-never-sick-lover

was sick.

Stood in front the glass doors
of my job's office building.
Frozen.
Fuck it. Those people can use the other doors.
Gray February skies mirrored the color within me.

Life goes on.

I wished you a speedy recovery and pushed open the
glass door.

The hours shivered by,
The computer screen blurred from 1-5pm.
Mumbles from coworkers crinkled and popped in my
ears.

Life goes on.

By 6:30 p.m., I hauled ass to the hospital you laid in.
Life didn't go on.
Not for me.
There was a pause.

Made sure you received your hot blankets, that your
bed was adjusted.
There was a pause.
A halt in the burning beneath my chest.
I was a hamster standing still as the wheel slowly
swung to a stop.
Couldn't sleep 'til you were home.
When you finally arrived, slumber gifted me some
relief.

Life goes on
Until my lover ain't well.

That's the day I realized just how important you are to
me.

Paper Factory Shenanigans

Camis and panties.
Ice chips on soft tits.
My lips on your clit.
Your hips, my fingertips.
Let's dip into the evening's sighs
and unstifled moans.
I am yours.
You are mine.

Cake at Paesano's

Date night in the concrete jungle.
Little Italy lookin' pretty during
that winter sunset.

Hearty hands locked as we strolled down
Mulberry with hard sole-clicks and fly-ass vans.
A fresh cut, giddy smile, hungry-belly-me.
Jittery arms, deep inhales, fluttered-belly-you.

Paesano's ambiance was captivating with the greenery,
paintings of nature, boats and impressionist lines.
Engraved woodwork that made me feel nice for
dining in there.

I didn't see it coming.

You said you got some cake and was nervous to give
me some.
I wanted the fucking slice of cake.

Entrees were delicious, drinks were strong as fuck.
I wanted my fucking cake. Was it chocolate mousse?
You right leg started to shake.

You eventually asked one of the servers to take a
picture of us.
I wanted the fucking cake.

You glided to my side of the table and kissed me
softly on my forehead.
"I have some cake for you." You smiled.
About. Fucking. Time.
I was instructed to close my eyes.
*Now, why T got this server standin' there? We supposed to be
takin' pictures.*
I closed them. Listened to my weighted triangle
earrings,
tambourine in my ears.

The surrounding gasps popped my eyes open
to find you down on one knee.
Heart was on speed demon, but my foundation was
on a steady stream.
"I went and got the cake. And I wanted to know if
you'll marry me."
Flabbergasted, I asked,
"So, this is the cake?"
Unified giggles and snickers,
you replied, "Yes,"
and I embraced you, my honey bun
with the extra glaze in the middle.
Fuck a slice of cake.

Smooth and Resilient

Early evening giggles and grins,
we spin our tongues to tales.
Foolishly, we show our skins,
bare our souls to each other as if
we never knew emotional baggage,
as if we never had war wounds from survival
busyness.
We love effortlessly.
Sun falls into Schuylkill River.
We finally decided to laugh at the bitter betties
bashing
our names for loving in the way that we do.
We still love effortlessly.
Through the midnight hour, we speak of gratitude,
thankful for inner child's play, the grace of being
grown.
We own our tales with easy groove in our mouths.
We love effortlessly.
Like shade was never thrown at our union.
Like our fears didn't claw at our connection.
Like our hearts didn't initially wanna run.
Like self-sabotage didn't wanna moisturize our
foundation for fun.
We love effortlessly.

Joyful and afraid, we give courage a new pair of eyes,
as we glide towards past skeletons,
call them out by name.
Dried up corpses will not separate us,
vanity will not become of us.
Purpose drips from our story.
Passion sops up the excess.

T, Da Deep Sea Diver

You make me river.
Shiver from soft caresses,
deep sea diver strokes.
You know how to swim in my waters.
You smile at my charted moans.
Every time I let you in a lil' deeper,
you take me higher.

Romance every spot,
until I gush like geysers.

Wet Romantic Strolls

Romantic strolls during the downpour.
Onlookers, peeking through blinds, don't need to understand
our watery giggles and intentional pauses drenched in release.
We bask in the mushy waters of a cloudy day and mundane conversation.

Seashore and Sand

Can I tell you about the time I fell in love with you in
seashore and sand?
Your hands shivering, cradling a camera, your lens
speak for you.
Artistic tongue, I watch in awe.
You got a knack for snagging portraits in captivating
off-guard-ness,
colorful emotions.
I saw you capture the color of joy that day.
It was breezy and barefoot,
in blue sky and sunrise hue.
As I breathed in ocean air, the flair of stillness
swaying up my spine,
I was reminded of how I love the water.
How it shushes my overthinking murmurs
And how I love you *in* passion.
In art.
In creativity.
You bend your knees, give seashells something to
vogue for.
Statuesque bones of former living things
are given a second chance in your lens.
And I watch in awe.
I wonder:

have you ever loved in seashore and sand?
You must have.
To paint in film in digitized notes of a moment…
You must have.
And that was the day I fell in love with you all over
again as you dug your feet into the sand,
with your camera in hand, ready to capture life's song
in still.

Maroon March I

I looked at my reflection,
excited to see my body draped in that orange baby
doll negligée.
Elated at your widened eyes and smile upon being
seen by you.
But the closer I got to the bed, the better I realized
how quick that
orange baby doll piece was going to be extracted.

Maroon March II

Body supported by a plump mattress,
plump ass cupped in my hands.
The plan was just to reconnect
after a stressful week,
to finally play with the thick maroon ribbons
folded in the upholstered box.
Eyes covered by the silk-feeling ribbon.
Your hands traced places that curved my back and my
chest was risen.
Your lips painted my canvas
in places that made my heaves deep and
my lips ready to cuss something good and filthy.
My head felt like it was spinning
because
who the fuck is you for me to trust you like this?
I guess *that* one
'cause my hands were willfully tied too.

Maroon March III

Within moments, words couldn't escape these lips.
I quivered from nibbles.
Gimme now, she cried.
You made her wait.
Lust so deep, my mind was immersed in playful
riddles.
Quizzically fisting my hands, wondering how deep
this kind of ecstasy would take us.
A little lick here, your pressed hand there,
love and passion everywhere.
Your scent.
Pulled me into you.
Foreplay in slow motion, while my yoni was coastin'
on impatience.
Gimme now, she cried.
You made her wait.
You gripped my inner thighs and had a feast I
couldn't run from,
a feast I couldn't witness,
but shit, we both enjoyed it.
More, she cried.
You tightened the ribbon around my hands
and gave her more.

Soulmate

We used to run,
let our hearts play hide-and-seek,
once vulnerability peeked through our lips, our eyes.
We've already seen each other's souls.
Our souls still laugh at our egos.
Oh, how we tried to guard ourselves
good and *well*
from a love so flowing.
A connection this deep didn't
need to break our walls.
It dug underground,
finessed our essences, until
we cried mercy to the passion.
Oh, how we tried to guard ourselves
good and *well*
from a love so flowing.
There's a skybridge between our hearts now.

Vegas, Epiphanies, Beige Coils

Our inner clocks were off,
our stresses gone.
That tangled beige coil of whataboutisms and
responsibilities straightened out as soon as we got off
the plane in Vegas.
Interesting how an evening flight
to a sin city desert would
clear our thoughts and raise our vibrations
to heights we hadn't sat in in a while.

Our inner clocks were off, and Denny's
was always down for our 4am breakfast.
Who would have thought a
chipper 4 a.m. Jasmine existed?
Don't answer.
                    Point is, *I ain't ever thought that shit.*
I did think of goals and plans with more sun on 'em
and the realization that:
Sometimes it isn't us.
                    It's our environment.
Our inner clocks were off,
but Vegas showed me that
the beige coil had no business inside of us.
The beige coil has no business inside of anyone,
really.
                    It was time for us to move.

Listenin' to Us

We kiss.
Saxophone riffs and smooth bass drape
the blackness of the moment.
Passion loves to intermingle in our hugs.
Tell me,
what do you hear when intimacy fills our room?
We know it already reeks of a love
I was told I couldn't have and a love they've
embraced to already know.
But tell me,
what do you hear when intimacy fills our room?

I'll tell you what I hear:
Melodic moans, breathy riffs, harmonies combine,
Within minutes of embracing, we know the baseline.
Intertwine our unique rhythms
creating a sound that curves my spine.
A song we love to play over
and over
        and over
and over
        and over again.

886

I told you: you gon' see.
From Brooklyn to Queens.
From Jersey to Philly,
we journeyed.
Still walking the path, side by side,
with Aubry struttin' in front
or behind.
Talking on the phone 'til the other falls asleep,
dancing in the house, slicing up vegetables while the
other seasons the meat.
Grooving while working, twerkin' acapella, writing
poems together.
Meditating in parks, homes and hotel rooms.
I love meditating with you.
Bickering, loud clapping while laughing,
teeth showing, crying in cuddles, dark seasons that
feel like a lifetime and a few more decades, popcorn
chicken hair and depression kicking ass. Whether
pockets are fat or wallets a lil' too slim, we still locked
in.
Tracing valleys, curves and soft mountains, long
kisses, short arguments about who that actor is on the
television—
Nah 'cause I saw her also on...Lemme check IMDb.

Vacations and annual AC trips.
Feet in sand, good food and quick pecks.
Growth and gains,
pull the other out of momentary pains.
Life can pull the rug from underneath us sometimes.
We got us though.
I told you: you gon' see.
Here we are.
At Love Park sharing words of long-term
commitment, loyalty and a love so mushy and tasty.
In white and pink and rainbow and queer.
We here.
In front of your mama, in front of my Daddy.
Siblings, aunties, uncles and a cousin too.
I love you.
My person.
Love of my life.
My heart adores you.
I still smile at the thought of you.
Still bashful when asking you out on dates.
Still giddy when I see you in various greens.
Still infatuated by the way you light up when talking
about your goals.
My heart still flutters the way you look at me.
This river ain't finna run dry for you, Baby.

But you know that now.

White Bootleg Converses in August

I choose you.
To love, trust and honor.
To lend you my ear and hold my lips tightly as you
relay the madness of your days or the blissful shifts
that light you up.
Hot damn, you look good when you glow.
I choose to stay open,
to continue to walk by your side and enjoy this life we
got.
To dance around the house with you 'til the end of
our days.
I won't give up on you, unless it requires giving up on
myself.

I will cherish your love, intellect and uniqueness.
Companion of my soul,
friend of my heart,
I come home to you.

LOVE

I married the love of my life at LOVE Park,
under the LOVE sculpture,
across the street from where we began
our journey full of inside jokes and LOVE.

Music and Rivers

Naked,
Open.
Kisses,
Satiny.
Heart beating rapidly to a deeper percussion.
Composure vanishes into the blackness
along with the forgotten playlist.
Caresses in acapella.
Thighs clinch your hips.
tambourinin' you slowly,
surrenderin' to the song of pleasure.
Embrace this vulnerability.
I'll receive your bare.
Respiring to the melody of your tongue
serenading my bosom, whining slow on my nipples.
My hands harmonize to the shape of your curves,
kiss the side of your neck.
I'm a wreck once you reach my pelvis.
Mmmm's resound beyond these four walls as
you taste these rivers for the umpteenth time.
But this time it's different.
You tapped into the stream bed without hesitation.
Gahhhh damn.
Give me what you got then.

Since you down there,

you hummin' a tune I've never heard before,

strokin' places, I've never felt before.

O 6 times.

Give me what you got then.

Kisses still satiny.

Hearts more open than they've ever been.

A symphony of our yellows,

a riff of our reds.

Lip bites to our orange,

give me what you got then.

O another 6 times.

Rhythm changes, but we're still so in sync.

Heavy breathing in rhyme.

Hip thrusts and grinds to our beat.

Time abandons our meter.

Close.

Grips.

Pins.

Pussy clenches, wraps around.

By the 8th O,

I couldn't even make a sound.

Keep givin' me what you got then.

Even If We Don't Make It

Sometimes,
I wonder if this will last 'til death do us part.
But I never wondered if this story of us is worth
telling.

         It's a page turner for sure.
Separation or not, it's a story I'll smile
softly to, while a summer breeze whizzes between my
dentures. Bones brittle but content to have the chance
to roam the land with you for a spell.
I would remember us sweetly.

This story is too good. Too delicious.

Reassurance

This love will not be like sand
slipping through our fingers.
It will not flat line.
Way beyond the tombstone,
our souls will intermingle.
Your hues of orange, my palette of purple,
our auras will love on.
Our spirits will thrive together.
Baby, this is a forever thing.

Winter Letter

If winter snow blankets over me first
and you miss me, know this:

It is an honor to love you.

To watch you shed layer after layer of heaviness that
kept you safe and pushed the unworthy away is
astounding.
I bow my head at the delicacy of your heart. Gift you
open arms when the world tries to destroy you for
being irrepressible.

If my heart has given in to a not fully understood
diagnosis and you wonder which parts I love about
you, remember this:

I love your hard. I love your soft. I love your
bold. I love your quiet. I love your voice. I love your
impatience. I love your patience. I love your hunger. I
love your chill. I love your passion. I love your
embrace. I love your light. I love your shadow. I love
your in-betweens, and I cherish your voice.

Every time I look into your eyes, it's like the first time
I saw them years ago when we were sitting by the
water. Moments of pausing, gawking at the warmth
of brown and the glisten from nearby lights.
When we laugh, my belly is full, my breath is thankful,
and my worries take a short getaway. When we hold
hands, I'm reminded of how priceless and
irreplaceable your being is.

If my time is up and no one saw it coming other than
Divine herself, know this:

  When I watch you create, my heart spins in
joy. I bite my lip when you discuss your dreams.
        You are large, T.
      Never forget that. Ever.

Your grit and aggression piss off the vampires, and
manipulators hate that your kindness has self-respect.
You know who you are.

If I should ever go first to sleep forever, remember
this:

Love of my life, I regret nothing being with you.
All seasons.
All moments.
All thoughts.
Every part of you, I love.

Use #OrangeSeptember with a picture or quote/s from the book.

Thanks for reading!

Orange September

ABOUT THE AUTHOR

Born and raised in New York, I'm a creative who found solace in poetry and short stories from a young age. With six published poetry collections and a debut novel, I explore themes of love, loss, life and self-discovery. After de-converting from Christianity, I embraced my late-blooming path and newfound freedom. I adore dancing in the kitchen, cherish time with loved ones, and find inspiration in books, travel, and live theater. Poetry is my first love and then short stories.

Personal Website:

http://www.jasminefarrell.com

Social Media:

Instagram: @authorjfarrell

Twitter: @jfarrellwrites